THE FOOTBALL TRIALS

DANGEROUS PLAY

BLOOMSBURY EDUCATION
Bloomsbury Publishing Plc
50 Bedford Square, London, WC1B 3DP, UK

First published in Great Britain 2018 by Bloomsbury Publishing Plc

A catalogue record for this book is available from the British Library

ISBN: PB: 978-1-4729-4415-3; ePDF: 978-1-4729-4416-0; ePub: 978-1-4729-4413-9

2 4 6 8 10 9 7 5 3 1

Cover design by James Fraser Design
Typeset by Integra Software Services Pvt. Ltd.

Printed and bound in China by Leo Paper Products.

To find out more about our authors and books visit
www.bloomsbury.com and sign up for our newsletters

recommended by

www.catchup.org

Catch Up is a charity which aims to address the problem of underachievement
that has its roots in literacy and numeracy difficulties.

THE FOOTBALL TRIALS
DANGEROUS PLAY

JOHN HICKMAN
Illustrated by **NEIL EVANS**

BLOOMSBURY EDUCATION

LONDON   OXFORD   NEW YORK   NEW DELHI   SYDNEY

CONTENTS

Lauren Fox   7

The Next Big Thing   15

The Walk Home   20

A Little Kiss   23

The Date   28

Forest   35

A Deal With the Devil   41

No Choices   48

Collared   54

Puppet   59

United   63

Watermelon   68

Lauren Fox

I look down at the ball at my feet. I don't need to look up at the goal; I already know where that is. Then I hit the ball. Hard and low, right across the keeper. It smashes against the post and into the net.

That's the hat-trick! The lads crowd around me and I'm absolutely buzzing.

After the game, even the Sunderland players congratulate me and Liam, my coach at United, throws his arm around me. "You keep playing like that," he tells me, "and the gaffer will have you in that first team in no time."

I still can't believe I play for United. It's only been a month since I signed schoolboy forms. It's unreal. Can you imagine? Me, playing in the Premier League? How amazing is that? But Liam is always banging on about how hard it is, how only the best players can make it and how we all need to get ourselves a proper education.

Life isn't that different. Other than getting double the homework – from school and United.

I have to do football training drills at home, whenever I get the chance. Plus I have to watch my diet. I've never eaten so many vegetables. Mum doesn't mind; she's been trying to get greens down me since I was little. Granddad keeps saying he's going to turn into a rabbit!

Mum and Granddad are waiting at the side of the pitch for me.

"Well done, Jackson," says Mum and she has this huge smile on her face.

"Just the three goals today then?" says Granddad.

"Didn't want to embarrass them," I tell him.

"You were totally brilliant," says Mum.

"All right, Mum, calm down," I tell her.

Ryan jogs over. "Are you going to Wheeler's place later?" he asks me.

"Definitely," I tell him.

"Sweet," he says. He nods at Granddad and jogs off.

"Partying tonight then?" asks Mum.

"If that's OK?" I ask.

"I think you've earned it," says Granddad.

After the game, I set off for Wheeler's place for the party. My head is still buzzing from the match. I give Wheeler's door a loud knock. Wheeler answers. "What's with all the banging? Thought you were the police!" he says.

In the living room, Ollie, Ryan, Jamal and Zeki from the academy are playing a footie game on the console.

"Ollie beating you again?" I ask Ryan.

"What do you think?" he answers.

Ollie grins at me. "Can't help being awesome," he says.

"Want a drink?" Wheeler asks me. "There's some cola in the fridge."

I grab a can, go back into the living room and watch Ollie score a worldie against Ryan.

Everyone is laughing when there's a knock at the door.

"Who could that be?" asks Wheeler, looking all shifty. He goes to the door.

After a moment, Amy from school comes in. Then Jade. The last girl through the door is Lauren Fox. My heart stops. What's she doing here?

I've had a thing for Lauren Fox since I knew what a "thing" was. I've known her since infant school. Our mums are friends and she used to come over and watch DVDs, and try and sit next to me on the settee. I didn't like it. I liked robots and dinosaurs and robot dinosaurs. Not girls. I thought girls had germs.

So whenever she sat next to me, I would get up and sit somewhere else. Then she would come and sit next to me again. And I would move again. I would pay money to have her sit next to me now though.

Everything about her is on point. Her hair is really dark, bobbed on one side and shaved down on the other. She's got these big brown sparkly eyes that I could stare into all day long.

She has a cute little stud in her nose. And an amazing smile. I mean, when she smiles, it's like she just lights up and my insides turn to goo. She's like the perfect combination of cool and cute and hot and...

"Jax man, stop staring," says Wheeler and drags me into the kitchen. He pulls open the fridge door and yanks out another can of cola.

"You never said Lauren was coming," I whisper.

"She isn't going out with Forest any more," he says.

My heart thuds. I'm not sure whether this is even better news than signing for United. "Since when?" I ask.

"Since... last week, I think," he says. "Are you going to ask her out?"

"OK, two problems," I say. "One. She would laugh at me. Two. What about Forest?"

"One. She wouldn't laugh," says Wheeler. "Two. Forget Forest."

"Like I can forget Forest," I say. "He would kill me."

"Here." He hands me another can. "We're going to talk to Lauren."

The Next Big Thing

Wheeler hands Amy and Jade their drinks. I give Lauren her can of cola. She smiles at me and I can feel myself getting all hot and itchy.

"Have you heard," says Wheeler, "about Jackson signing for United?"

"Yeah," says Lauren. "That's so cool."

"You could be his WAG!" says Wheeler.

I can feel myself melting with embarrassment. But Lauren just laughs and it's not a mickey-taking laugh. Doesn't seem like it anyway. It seems like a nice, sweet, warm laugh.

"So what happened with Forest, then?" asks Wheeler.

"It's over," she says.

"Why?" asks Wheeler.

"You're too nosy," I tell him.

"It's OK," says Lauren. "He was an idiot. I'm sick of idiots."

"Bad luck, Jax," Wheeler says. "That counts you out!"

I frown and shake my head.

"Just playing," says Wheeler. "Jax is a top boy. Now..." He puts his arms around Amy and Jade. "Let's get some tunes on, ladies." He winks at me and leads them away.

"So," says Lauren.

"So," I say back. I grin. Sort of. I glance over at Ollie and Ryan. They're both watching me, smirking, waiting for me to make an idiot of myself.

Ryan nods at me, as if to say, "Go on then, let's see what you're made of."

Dance music plays from Wheeler's speakers.

"So the United thing," she says. "You must be buzzing?"

"Yeah," I tell her. "It's just..."

"What?"

"Just scared I'll mess it up," I say.

"You won't," she says. "I've seen you play. You're really good."

A big smile fills my face. "You reckon?"

"Yeah," she says. "Do you remember when I used to come over to your house? When we were little?"

"A bit," I lie.

"It's weird," she says, "how long we've known each other."

"I know, yeah," I say.

She smiles at me and I smile back awkwardly. Then I turn away from her. She's so fit. I can't bear to look at her for too long. It's like looking at the sun or something. I should tell her that. Actually, no. That's lame. I should never tell anyone that. Ever.

I know I should ask her out. I should just say, "So what are you doing tomorrow night?" That's what Wheeler would say. But I'm terrified my words won't come out properly and will end up sounding nothing like words at all.

"Lauren," says Amy. She takes Lauren's hand. "I need you a minute!" And she drags Lauren away before I can even try and say something.

The Walk Home

For the rest of the night, I wait for a chance to talk to Lauren again. The problem is, the moment doesn't seem to come. If she's not talking with Amy, she's talking with Jade. Or Ollie, or Ryan.

Everyone wants to know what happened between her and Forest.

Then I hear Lauren tell Amy and Jade she has to go and see her give them both hugs.

Wheeler nudges me. "You're missing your chance." Before I can say anything, Wheeler calls out to Lauren. "Jax will walk you home," he says.

"You don't have to walk with me, you know," says Lauren, as we go along Wheeler's street. "I'm a big girl."

"I don't mind," I tell her.

We don't say much else and suddenly we're outside Lauren's house. I wish she lived miles away, so we could just walk together all night.

"Thanks," she says. She smiles.

We both stand there in silence for like a full five seconds.

I know I should ask her out or something, but I really don't know how.

"Give me your phone," she says.

"What for?" I ask.

"Duh, so I can get your number," she says.

This is why I didn't want to speak. "Yeah, duh," I say. I slip my hand into my pocket and pull my phone out. My hands are shaking. I type in the unlock code. The wrong code. "Just a sec," I say. After my second attempt, I manage to unlock my phone and hand it to her.

She types in a number. "I'll prank myself," she says. She lets the phone ring and ends the call. She hands my phone back. "Night then." She walks up her path.

I wait until she's inside before I go. At the end of her street, I check there's no one around. Then I blast an imaginary football into an imaginary goal!

A Little Kiss

The next day, Wheeler calls for me and the pair of us play a game we call squash. We each take a turn to whack the football against the wall at the back of the flats.

Wheeler smacks the ball hard against the bricks. I'm surprised the wall doesn't crumble with those hefty boots of his.

"This United thing," he says. "You're going to have to think about representation."

"What you on about?" I ask. I smack the ball against the wall.

"You need an agent," he says. He boots the ball again. "I could do it, if you wanted?"

"You could be my agent?" I ask.

"Yeah," he says. "Why not?"

Before I can answer, my phone beeps in my pocket. I pull it out. "It's Lauren," I tell Wheeler.

He laughs and pats me on the back. "Nice one. What does it say?"

It says, "Hey how r u? x"

"There's a kiss," says Wheeler.

"What shall I say back?" I ask.

"You need to ask her something," he tells me. "Ask her how she's been or something."

I type my message: "I'm good, how r u?"

"Should I put a kiss?" I ask Wheeler.

"A big one," says Wheeler.

I add a big X to the text. "That OK, you reckon?" I show Wheeler the text.

"It will do," he says. "For you."

I send the message.

"How long do you think I should give her to reply?" I ask.

"Look," says Wheeler. "If she gets back to you straight away, she's proper into you. If she takes a few hours, she's interested, but she's busy. Anything longer than a day, she's just being nice. Forget about it."

"How do you know all these things?" I ask.

"I've had a lot of experience," he says. "And I've watched a few of those soppy, romantic films girls like. Don't tell anyone. Just between us, yeah?"

My phone beeps again. I pull it out. Another message from Lauren. I stare at Wheeler while my heart bounces about inside me. I read it out to him. "It says, 'I'm good thanks. What you up to tonight?'"

The Date

I stare at my phone. Just after seven. I had arranged to meet Lauren outside the McDonalds in town at seven. Been standing here since half six. I was so nervous I was just walking backwards and forwards at home.

Granddad told me to clear off, before I wore a hole in the carpet.

Someone taps me on my shoulder.

I spin around. Lauren is standing there. She looks stunning. Her hair is looking proper nice, all done up and she's got these round Harry Potter glasses on that would look ridiculous on most people. But she just looks awesome. She has on a stripy top, leggings and sneakers. She doesn't even have to try. She could rock up in Mum's supermarket uniform and look amazing.

And then she smiles at me and I can feel my insides melting. Like actually melting. I get why people get all mushy when they like someone. It's because their insides literally turn to mush.

"Been waiting long?" she asks.

"No," I lie. "Just a few minutes."

As we walk through town my nerves really kick in. What if she doesn't like me? What if she does? What if someone sees us? What if they tell Forest? Worse still, what if we see Forest?

Once we're in the cinema, I get us tickets for some horror film neither of us has heard of. I don't care what we watch. All I'm interested in is hanging out with Lauren. We could watch a washing machine on a spin cycle and I would be happy.

The cinema is almost empty, which is cool. I would rather it was just me and Lauren. Fewer people to spot us. But also, fewer people to see if I really embarrass myself and get a slap.

I have no idea what I'm going to do that will make Lauren slap me, but I'm terrified that I might do something stupid and mess things up.

We have the whole middle row to ourselves.

Lauren offers me some popcorn from her huge bag. I take a handful and smile at her.

Then the movie starts. On screen, there are people at a Halloween party, doing a Ouija board.

"This is going to go badly," I whisper.

"Totally," she says.

All I really want is to put my arm around Lauren. Problem is, I don't know how. I mean I know how putting my arm around someone works, obviously. I just don't how to start it off. So I don't do anything. I just sit there as the movie plays.

And before I know it, we're sitting on the bus heading home.

The bus pulls up at Lauren's stop and I suddenly feel the need to do something. Now or never.

"I'll walk you back, if you want?" I tell her.

"If you want," she says.

We get off the bus and walk along. I'm going to do it this time, I say to myself. I'm going to grab her and kiss her.

I don't care what happens. OK, I do care. I don't want to hurt her when I grab her or anything. I'm just going to kiss her. Though I need to make sure I don't bump heads with her. Or knock her glasses off. Or something embarrassing.

"Oh no," says Lauren.

"What?" I ask. For a moment I wonder whether she can read my mind and she knows I'm thinking about bumping her head or knocking her glasses off.

"Forest," she says.

Oh no.

Forest

There aren't many people who scare me, but
Forest is one of them. He's built like a tank
and the veins pop out of his forearms like he's
always doing weights. But that's not the thing.
The thing is he's evil.

I think that most people have some good and bad in them. But Forest, I'm not so sure. I think he might just be all bad.

Forest heads towards us, hood up. His sidekicks, Buff and Chenner are right behind him. It amazes me Forest has any friends. There's no way they can actually like him. I bet even his own mum doesn't like him.

"Loz," snaps Forest. "What do you think you're doing?" He's talking to Lauren, but he's giving me a dirty look.

"What are you on about?" asks Lauren.

"I want to know what you're doing," he says. "With **him**."

A shiver goes down my spine. I'm pretty certain he tortures animals. That's the first sign of a murderer, isn't it? Drowning kittens. Kicking puppies.

"You can't tell me what to do," she says. "Not any more."

Forest stares at me again. "So you're choosing him over me?"

I want to say something, but I'm proper scared. So I just stand there and say nothing, like an idiot.

"This has got nothing to do with Jax, or anyone else," says Lauren. "This is about me and you."

"Yeah," says Forest. "Me and you."

"It's over," she says. "Me and you. It's over."

Forest stares at me like this is all my fault. "We'll see," he says. "Come."

He flicks his head and his mates follow him. He bumps into me as he passes, almost knocking me over.

Me and Lauren stand there for ages, waiting for them to be properly gone, before either of us says anything.

"I'm sorry," says Lauren.

"I don't get it," I say. "You're so nice. I don't get how you could go out with someone like Forest."

"I thought there was a different side to him," she tells me.

"Is there?" I ask.

"If there is, it's buried so deep no one will ever find it." She kisses me on the cheek. "Night, Jax."

And then she's gone.

And I've got this horrible feeling that my chance with Lauren has gone too.

Even if she actually liked me, Forest has seen to that. I really wish I had let her sit next to me when we were little. Things might have worked out different.

I walk to the end of Lauren's street. Then I look both ways.

I'm not worried about getting hit by cars. I'm worried about getting hit by Forest. I just know he will be waiting around some corner for me.

I don't walk home. I run. As fast as I can. All the way.

A Deal with the Devil

A couple of days later, I'm on my way to training. All the way to the bus stop, I keep looking behind me. This stuff with Forest has got me really stressed. It doesn't matter what I'm thinking about, he's always there, at the back of my mind.

It's like he's watching over me. The worrying thing is, I can actually imagine him standing over me in the middle of the night. With an axe in one hand and a chopped off head in the other. I know – I've seen too many horror films. I should probably watch some of those soppy, romantic films Wheeler loves so much, where he gets all his hints about how girls' minds work.

But Forest doesn't jump out on me and I get to Samuels Park without being attacked. At training, Liam sorts us into two teams and we have a kick about. I'm on the same side as Ryan and Ollie which is cool with me. We make a pretty good team.

The problem is my head is all over the place, with Lauren and Forest. Which means my feet are all over the place too!

Ryan bursts through from defence with the ball and slides the ball across the goal. It's a tap-in. All I have to do is get a toe on it. And I do. Right over the bar. I fall onto the grass like someone has shot me. Pretty embarrassing. I pick myself up and wipe the grass from my T-shirt. I can see Ryan, smiling, shaking his head.

"Good effort," he says sarcastically.

I grunt, take it on the chin. "Thanks."

On the way home from training, I'm still embarrassed about that miss. The lads are never going to let me forget it.

"Yo!" someone shouts.

I spin around. Before I can do anything, Forest has me by the neck, pushed against a wall. His face is red and angry.

My heart is thumping.

"Thought you could get with my girl?" he spits.

I try and say something, but my words don't come out right. "D-d-don't..."

Buff mimics me, standing behind Forest. "D-d-don't hurt me."

"I'm going to hurt him," says Forest. He lifts his fist, ready to throw it at my face.

"Wait," says Chenner. "I've got a better idea. If he's playing for United, I bet the kids down there are minted."

"So?" says Forest.

"So," says Chenner, "let's get him doing a bit of work for us."

"Yeah OK," says Forest. "I want you to nick all you can for me – phones, watches, whatever. When have you got your next game?"

I stare at the ground.

He grabs me by the cheeks and squeezes my face. "Look at me when I'm talking. When is your next game?"

"Sunday," I say, pushing the word through my squashed up lips.

He lets go of my face. "We'll be waiting outside the gates."

Suddenly, he swings a fist into my gut.

A pain shoots through me, making me double up.

"You tell anyone, it won't just be you I come for, you get me?" Forest says. "I know where your girlfriend lives, remember?" Then he pushes me away. "Come, boys," he says.

Forest and his mates walk off, laughing and joking, like this is all some funny game.

I watch them go, clutching my belly. I hate him so much. But I have to do what he says, if he's going to hurt Lauren.

I can't let that happen.

No Choices

As Sunday's game gets closer, I work out that I have two choices. I rob the changing rooms and get booted out of United. Or I don't and I'm dead. And Lauren gets hurt too.

As much as I want to play for United, I can't let anything bad happen to Lauren. There is a third choice. I rob the changing rooms, deal with Forest and get away with it. The thing is, I'm not that lucky. And anyway, when people found out their stuff had been nicked, I would be the prime suspect. Rough kid from a rough estate. Just the way it is.

I turn up at Samuels Park on Sunday morning for the match. All I want to think about is football, but all I can really think about is Forest and what he's making me do. I don't say a word to anyone in the changing rooms, not even Ollie.

How can I? He won't want anything to do with me when he finds out what I'm planning to do.

Out on the field, the parents are lined up on the touchline. Wonder what they'll say about me when they hear I've stolen from their sons. Mum and Granddad aren't watching the game. They wanted to but I told them it made me more nervous when they were watching.

Truth is, I would love to have them here. I just couldn't risk them getting caught in the crossfire of my beef with Forest. I didn't even tell Wheeler about any of it. Haven't told anyone.

I tell Liam I'm not feeling right and he switches me out for Zeki, one of the subs. I'm surprised to see Ryan is a sub too, but he says he felt a bit of a strain in his thigh and didn't want to risk an injury.

I watch from the sidelines as the game kicks off. Straight away, Ollie is bossing it in midfield, spraying passes all over the pitch. No one on the other team can get close to him.

With about fifteen minutes gone, we get a corner. Zeki swings one in and their defender heads it clear. Ollie picks it up on the edge of the area. He controls it with his right, then moves it onto his left. He hits the ball. It curls, right into the top corner. An absolute worldie. Everyone goes crazy, the whole team crowds around him.

With everyone celebrating, I grab my chance. I take a look behind me, before I go into the changing rooms. No one is around.

I go over to Jamal's stuff and reach inside his coat pockets. I pull out a phone. I feel proper sick when I see his background – the United badge.

"What are you doing?" asks someone from behind me.

I spin around.

Ryan is standing there. He points at the phone in my hand. "What have you got that for?"

Collared

I think about lying to him, but I don't. "I was going to nick it," I say. I don't know why I'm telling Ryan the truth, but it feels good to get it off my chest.

"What for?" he asks.

I take a breath. "This kid. Forest. He's scary. Worse than you."

Ryan laughs.

"Not even joking," I tell him. "I mean, proper crazy. He said if I didn't rob this place, he was going to hurt this girl."

"What girl?" Ryan asks.

"Lauren," I say, "from the party."

"What's his problem?" he asks.

"She's his ex," I tell him.

"Oh," he says. "And you're getting with her?"

"Maybe," I say. "I don't even know."

"So, what are you going to do?" he asks.

"No choice," I tell him. "Forest said he would be waiting for me outside the gates."

"You should tell someone," Ryan says.

"As if," I say. "What about you? Are you going to tell Liam?"

"Tell him what?" he asks.

"About this? About the phone?" I say.

"What phone?" he asks.

I give him a nod. I've not known Ryan long, and when I first met him he was a proper idiot. But he's OK.

"I'll catch you later," says Ryan. Then he walks out.

I grab the phone. A couple of other phones too. And a tablet. I stuff the gear into the bottom of my backpack, covering it with my clothes. Never stolen anything in my life before. I feel proper lousy.

After the match, I don't go into the changing room. I just rush straight out of the academy building. Outside, the sky is grey. It looks like rain. I hope Forest isn't waiting for me.

I hope he forgot our deal or found something more interesting to do. Or better still, perhaps he's been hit by a car.

My heart sinks. I'm the one who feels like he's been hit by a car.

Forest is standing at the gates with Buff and Chenner, just like he said they would be.

Puppet

I think about running back inside the academy building, but there's no point. I would just be putting it off. Making it worse. I need to get it over and done with.

Then, I can just go back to normal. Maybe United won't press charges when they find out what I've done.

Forest stares at me. Then he flicks his head, wanting me to follow him around to the side of the gate, so we're out of sight. Perfect place for a shady deal.

"Surprised you've shown up," says Forest. "You got the stuff?"

I pull my backpack off my shoulder and unzip it.

Forest buries his face in the bag like a pig in a trough. He sees the phones. Then he hands the bag to his mates. "Not bad," he says. "Think we might have to make this a regular thing."

My skin goes cold. "I... I can't," I tell him.

Forest grabs me by the neck. "I haven't forgotten what you've done, you know."

This is worse than I imagined. I thought that when I gave the gear to him, that would be it. But it's not, is it? I'm going to be his puppet for as long as wants.

"They'll kick me out," I tell him. "When they find out that I've robbed the place."

Forest gives me a nasty look. "Then you had better make sure they don't find out."

I think about Ryan. What he saw. What I told him. "But they might," I say. "They already know I'm trouble."

"Trouble?" asks Forest. "What do you mean?"

"You don't... know me very well," I say. "I don't do as I'm told."

Forest grabs me by the neck. His ugly, fat face is right next to mine. "Remember that punch in the stomach I gave you?" he asks with a nasty smile. "Well, there's plenty more where that came from, if you don't do as you're told."

United

I want to swallow, but I'm scared of getting punched if I move. So I don't move a muscle. My heart thumps in my chest. This is where my story ends. All of it over, before it's even begun.

I close my eyes.

Then I hear something.

Footsteps on concrete. People running.

"GET OFF HIM!" shouts someone.

I open my eyes and manage to twist my neck to see the lads standing there. My team. Ollie, Ryan, Jamal, Angel, Indy, Zeki... The WHOLE team. Everyone.

"Get off him, now," orders Ryan.

"Or what?" asks Forest.

"Or we kick your head in," Ryan tells him.

Forest stares at Ryan for ages. Then he nods at Buff and Chenner.

They let me go.

I back away from Forest, towards my team-mates. I turn to Ryan. "What... what are you doing?"

"I can give you grief," he says. "But no one else can. No one messes with one of my team."

I feel powerful. Like a general with an army behind him.

"Has he told you what he's done?" shouts Forest. "Robbing from you all."

"Yeah, what **you** made him do," says Ryan.

I look around at them.

"Don't sweat it," says Jamal. "We know it wasn't your fault."

I want to make this right, but I'm scared. Really scared. "Give me the bag," I tell Forest.

He looks at me with hatred. Shakes his head.

"Do it," says Ryan.

Forest swears at us, then he hands the bag over. "I won't forget this," he says to me.

"Neither will we," says Ryan. "If I find out you're giving my boy any more aggro, I'll come find you. You get me?"

Forest's eyes are burning with anger but he looks around at his mates and flicks his head.

The three of them turn around and walk away.

I grab the stolen gear from my backpack and hand it back to the lads who I took it from. "Sorry," I say again. I look at Ryan. "Cheers, man."

"You're part of the team," he says. "We stick together."

Watermelon

I lie on my bed thinking about the last few days. What's happened, what's going to happen. Why can't things just be simple?

The intercom buzzes.

Mum is out and Granddad is watching TV, so I roll off my bed and go and answer it. "Hello?" I say.

"Hey, Jax, it's Lauren."

My heart beats fast and I can't stop myself from smiling. "Come up," I tell her. I buzz her in and wait. I listen as the lift clanks about. Then, after what seems like forever, the lift doors open and Lauren is standing there.

"You want to come in?" I ask.

"No, it's fine, we can just stand here in this cold corridor," she says with a smile.

I stare at her. "What, really?"

"No, of course not," she says. "Obviously I want to come in!"

I laugh at my lameness and lead her into my bedroom.

"I know what happened," she says. "Ryan texted me." She takes my hand. "I'm sorry," she whispers.

"Not your fault," I tell her.

"Forest is such an idiot," she says.

"He told me he would hurt you," I say. I leave out the part that he said he would kick my head in too. Makes me seem less of a hero.

"You're so sweet," she says. Then she gently puts her hand on my cheek and turns my head so I'm facing her. She closes her eyes and leans in.

She kisses me.

I close my eyes too. Her lips are warm and moist and taste of watermelon. Oh wow. All the hassle, all the drama. Worth it. One hundred per cent.

Inside I want to jump and cheer like United have just scored a last minute winner. But I don't. That would be incredibly lame.

We move apart and I lick my lips. Can still taste watermelon. I think I now have a new favourite fruit.

"You OK with me sitting next to you now then?" asks Lauren. "You always used to get up and sit somewhere else."

I shake my head and smile. "Yeah," I tell her. "You can sit next to me."

Bonus Bits!

Football Words

Here are some examples of football jargon that are used in the book. Did you know what they all meant?

Gaffer the person who is in charge of the team (the manager)

Worldie a world class goal

WAG Wives and Girlfriends (of the football players)

Quiz Time!

Why not test your knowledge with these multiple choice questions? Refer back to the story if you need to. There are answers at the end (but no peeking!)

1. Why does Granddad say he is going to turn into a rabbit?

   A his teeth have grown really long

   B he is eating lots of greens

   C he has big ears

   D he is eating lots of nuts

2. Who does Wheeler think is at the door when Jackson knocks on it?

   A his dad

   B Ryan

   C the police

   D his teacher

3. What colour are Lauren Fox's eyes?

   A blue

   B green

   C brown

   D hazel

4. What time does Jackson arrive for his date with Lauren?

   A 6.30 pm

   B 6.45 pm

   C 7.00 pm

   D 7.15 pm

5. What does Forest call Lauren?

   A Lauren

   B Loz

   C Laura

   D Len

6. Who sees Jackson take Jamal's phone?

   A the gaffer

   B Forest

   C Ryan

   D Jamal

7. How does Jackson feel when his team arrives to get rid of Forest?

   A like a general

   B like a thief

   C like a football manager

   D like a police officer

8. What do Lauren's lips taste of?

   A blueberry

   B vanilla

   C strawberry

   D watermelon

Think about it

Jackson has to make some tough decisions in this story.

- Why do you think Jackson worries about Forest?
- Would you have done what Forest asked Jackson to do? Why/why not?
- How do you think Ryan feels towards Jackson when he sees him taking the phone?
- What about when he sees Jackson giving the phones to Forest?

ANSWERS TO 'QUIZ TIME!'

1B, 2C, 3C, 4A, 5B, 6C, 7A, 8D

Look out for more of Jackson's adventures!

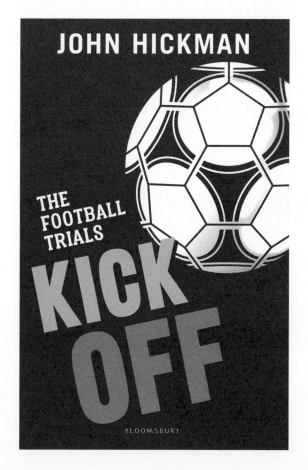

978-1-4729-4411-5

For more news and information about

Bloomsbury's High Low books visit

www.bloomsbury.com